DOORIYAN

A JOURNEY OF SOULMATES

PEARL VOHRA BHATIA

Made with ♥ on the Notion Press Platform
www.notionpress.com

This book is dedicated to my family, who always supported and encouraged me to follow my passion of writing.

Thanks Ma & Pa

Contents

Preface

This story is about one of my best friend's love life. The two estranged persons who met as strangers but ended up loving and adoring each other madly. Their journey from unknowns to soulmates is something I have always adored and admired. Initially I used to hate the very fact that my friend Pia who is an average looking girl, can be loved by someone so madly... But then I realised that he is her true soulmate... they are just made for each other... else how was it possible that coming from two distant family backgrounds, careers, cities and interests they met each other and even rose in love. They never fell in love with each other, they always rose in their love and blossomed with every passing day. They faced difficulties, they had differences, they fought but never parted their ways. The journey began as strangers, went as friends, going on as lovers with no end of this voyage. I still remember how they interacted for the first time and met each other to be life partners...

Prologue

Hello Friends,

This book is about something very personal, something which has changed my life eternally. This book is about two communities, two cultures, two states, two families and one feeling... LOVE. This book would let you experience the power love has, the struggles love faces, the changes it undergoes, the pain it gives and the happiness it bestows.

While I was thinking of penning down my first book, I recalled each and every moment Pia experienced during her courtship period with Ray - her lover, friend, mentor, companion, ... in short everything. He taught her, he loved her, he hated her, he preceded her, he betrayed her, he annoyed her, he even made her laugh... they shared every emotion with each other and became soulmates.

The couple was destined, and they knew this, the very day they fell for each other. They met through an unbelievable incident or should I say, a chain of incidents. But the day they met, Pia knew they are made for each other, Love at First Sight! Although, Ray took his leisure time to realise this very own fact, but yes he did realise.

I am not going to bore you guys anymore, let's start with this beautiful journey full of hardships.

Author

CHAPTER ONE

THE FIRST INTERACTION

The keys on the keyboard are making wonderful music, while there is a lot of noise and chaos in the background. The chit - chat among the office colleagues is pretty normal, however, Pia loves to involve herself in her work. She is being referred to as Workaholic sometimes by her colleagues, but that does not bother her as she wants to be a great Marketer one day.

"Pia, get some break dear you are too young to work so hard," said Kajal. "I am fine dear, you keep it up I don't mind" Pia replied with a smirk on her face. Pia never interacted much with Kajal or with any of her colleagues for that matter. She loves to concentrate on her work and learning.

"Hey, Pia come, let's go for lunch. I am hungry, da" Anaya said while walking towards Pia to move her away from the system. "Bosy, why do you always do this to me? You know na when I am working I don't like to be disturbed," Pia childishly told Anaya.

Pia is Anaya's junior but has never been treated like one by Anaya. The entire office claims them to be best friends. Anaya interviewed Pia and liked her writing skills as well as her confidence. Pia is the youngest of all the 300 employees at Global Communications.

Pia was engrossed in her work as usual, when a phone call from an unknown number distracted her from an important presentation. She answers casually to that unknown number, but to her surprise the guy strangely calls him, her friend and she disconnects the phone call to carry on with her presentation. Days passed by, Pia had almost forgotten that unknown number call, when suddenly she received a friendship message from that same number at 12 midnight. Ignoring the same, she deletes the message and goes to sleep. Then there follows a sequence of messages for the next few days, irritated with all this she shouts at that person and warns him of police complaint. With no fear of that warning, the stranger keeps messaging Pia and gives her a call on the New Year's eve to wish her a happy and prosperous year ahead. She shares this with her younger sister and then on enquiry she gets to know that the stranger is her friend's cousin who has this sweet name, Ray.

Days, weeks and months passed by there was no link left between Pia and Ray. Both were strangely busy in their lives desolated of each other. Few days past, Pia's birthday and Ray texted her wishing her a belated birthday. Strangely they interacted this time and shared some jokes among themselves. Then there was an exchange of a few such casual conversations between them via Gtalk and Facebook. After months of chatting and telephonic conversations, they decided to meet up with each other. This meeting came as a destiny's mandate since, both of them became an integral part of each other's life.

Ray, who was known for his non-texting skills got stuck to his phone's keypad texting Pia all the time. His friends started teasing him but he was undisturbed with all those statements as he felt this, as was his need of texting her. He would now wait for her call in the morning to wake him up, give her a call when he leaves for his college and during breaks. Text her during lectures, travel, friends' hang-out. Pia was all over in Ray's life now.

The other side was also a similar situation. Pia who never ever bothered to interact with any guy in her college or office started caring about someone unknown and stranger. She had a weird habit of not calling back to her missed calls but for Ray, she not only calls him back but eagerly waits for his calls. There was a kinda schedule of conversation between them and no matter what, they both always adhered to the same intentionally / unintentionally.

After long unmet interactions and delays, the day of the meeting arrives. Pia has to come after attending her college and Ray would come from his home. At around 12 in the noon Pia calls up Ray to confirm the meeting, but her unanswered calls from Ray's end disturbs her. She keeps on calling him till he receives the call and says that he would need half an hour to reach the meeting place. And finally they meet @ Rajeev Chowk Metro station, New Delhi.

But this meeting was not as easy as it sounds, Pia had to wait for half an hour to meet her "Destined Friend - Ray". Yes you read it right, half an hour, watching people rushing in hurry to board / deboard metro, peeping into Cafe Coffee Day's menu, looking at the time every minute... that moment she must have realised the importance of seconds even. I was surprised to know this and was wondering why would anybody wait for Half An Hour to meet some stranger... but could not get my answer till date.

Well after such a long wait, Pia finally met Ray, they both were a bit shy in initiating the conversation, then Pia asked him if he had come alone to meet her? Ray, as his nature jokingly said no.. no.. I am not alone, my friends are scattered everywhere in the station.... and they both shared a good laughs...

CHAPTER TWO

THE UNKNOWN RELATION

Their texting used to long for hours, they began sharing their daily routine micro details with each other. The strange part was, none would ask the other about the day's event but it was like a self call of sharing everything. Pia would tell Ray about everything, and he would even listen with patience though he understood little. Ray on the other hand, would share the good and positive things about the daily routine, he never shared his problems and issues with Pia. This sometimes had them arguing with each other, where both were right on their parts. Pia would poke Ray so that he shares his problems with her but he would restrain himself as he did not want Pia to think more about him.

Their texts now became informal and more friendly, their chats now had friendly teasing and a bit of flirt. Their equation was different and unique so much so that they rarely used words to express themselves, their expressions were enough to talk and express. There was an unusual bonding between both of them, which I could never understand.

I guess it was that bonding only, which energised unwell Pia to travel all the way to Noida from Gurgaon to meet Ray.

She was not even able to walk, but since their meeting was already planned, she took medicine and went to meet him. This gesture of hers, surprised Ray and he got some idea about Pia's feelings for him but never expressed. Pia on the other side, was still figuring out what is all this???

To all this, added up a remarkable incident which changed their equation all together. One fine day, early morning Ray texted Pia that he wants to meet her now. This message came as a surprising element for her, as they had decided none would msg so early... She replies back to him to know what's the matter... Furious and agitated Ray reverts for the meeting at Cafe Coffee Day @ Rajeev Chowk Metro Station. Dunno why, but Pia that day bunked her college to meet him. The moment she reaches the meeting place, she is surprised to see Ray who was waiting for her for the past one hour. She exclamatory asked him what on the earth was so urgent that he wanted to meet her immediately... Smiling Ray says that he wanted to show her how he looks in anger so that she knows him better. That day, they both came much closer than earlier, spent the entire day together, roamed around the city, attended book fair, drank coffee, ate lunch and did all sorts of nuisances. I asked her if she was in love with Ray, but Pia refused to it saying that they are just good friends. But I was convinced that Pia has started liking Ray and vice-versa and told Pia let's wait and watch if it is *just a friendship or something else.*

My statement brought confusion to Pia's mind and she started thinking over it, when Ray comforted her saying there is nothing like that from either side. That day Pia smiled, laughed and was happy more than she was ever...

Days went by, Pia had a college trip and had to leave for Puducherry, she wanted to talk to Ray once before leaving the town, but was unable to connect as Ray's phone was not reachable. During the 25 hours train journey, Pia was constantly looking for a network so that she could talk to Ray. On reaching Pondicherry, she tried connecting to him but failed. Then annoyingly she texted her cousin asking Ray to call her immediately. That day, around 8 p.m. Pia gets a call from an unknown number, on receiving call she hears Ray's voice and starts to shout at him for his carelessness and ignorance towards her. Ray calmed her down and told her that he texted her on facebook and left msg on Gtalk as well that he has lost his phone. That was Pia's 3rd day in Puducherry, when the entire night she had a conversation with Ray. She shared her experiences and told him everything about the trip.

Now, every night they both used to talk over phone for hours from evening to night till morning. Both had sleepless nights just to talk to each other and share their lives more closely and deeply.

They used to talk on anything to everything from their past to careers to movies to sex to everything one could think of on this Earth. Pia had never had such a relationship with anyone else before, she was more than comfortable with Ray and felt secure even if he is not physically present. His thought would keep hovering in her mind, the moment she would feel good, bad, lonely, crowded, happy, romantic, sad or even ditched she would pick her phone up and call up Ray to share her feelings.

Even in a drunken state she was comfortable in talking to him, as she knew somewhere that there is a special bond that they both share. But what is this... this bond... this was as unknown as a stranger...

CHAPTER THREE

THE STRANGE PROPOSAL

After 12 days of Puducherry trip, while returning to her hometown, Pia called up Ray to tell him that she is coming back. She boarded the train along with her college mates at around 9:00 p.m. from Chennai station on 18th of April to reach New Delhi station at 7:30 a.m. on 20th of April. The entire journey of hers went either talking to Ray or thinking about him. Similar was the situation of Ray, he had sleepless nights with the entire day texting Pia and knowing her whereabouts.

On the 19th morning, after talking to Ray, Pia had a severe stomach ache. Then unbearable, she started screaming Ray's name. Her friends were surprised as they had no idea of what's wrong with her. Calling a doctor they discovered that she ate something wrong due to which she had that pain. The doc gave her medicine and she went to sleep on some relief. During this time, Ray called her up a number of times with some texts unreplied. In the evening, when she woke up, she saw her phone and immediately called up Ray.

On knowing the entire episode of her pain, Ray asked if she is better now and asked her to stay in touch with him every moment of her train journey, till she reaches her home. Now, the entire journey went by on phone calls or texts. The network during train journeys, as we all know is an on - off scenario, still they both had patience and kept talking to each other.

That night they both were emotionally together and lovers. They now wanted to be together for all their lifetime, though this thought / feeling was first confessed by Pia.

Yes, Pia... she had always believed that why should always a guy propose to a girl, if she was in love with someone she would not wait for that person to come and propose to her. And she did exactly the same that night. She confessed her true feelings to Ray, "*Ray, I think I have started liking you more and more... this is not just liking this is more than that... this is love yes love... I love you Ray*"

This statement of hers, stunned Ray, he could not speak a single word for minutes and the phone got disconnected. This time Pia did not call back, as she thought Ray did not like what she said. She was feeling guilty of confessing her feelings to Ray and losing a great friend of hers. But what she did not know was the fact that Ray could not believe that Pia is too honest towards him and her feelings. Her honest and soulful confession had taken him in surprise.

After a few hours, Ray called up Pia to say, "*Pia, I like you too. I have felt like pampering you. I want to feel your breath and be with you always*".

They both went to sleep at around 5:00 a.m on 20th when the train was about to reach Delhi in another couple of hours. On reaching New Delhi Station, Pia's friend woke her up to get down of the train. On de-boarding the train, she gets a call from Ray who is waiting for her at the metro station to accompany her till MG Road Metro station.

She hastily walks down to the metro station with her friends, but leaves them to meet Ray. She curiously waits for him to come but could not find him, meanwhile Ray keeps watching her from behind a pillar. He calls her and surprises her by complimenting her that she is looking beautiful in that green and blue dress. She looks here and there to find him but fails to see him, when all of a sudden he appears in front of her and astonishes her.

She hugs him and thanks him for coming with a lowered tone, " *I love You*"...

CHAPTER FOUR

THE MEETINGS ON - OFF

After the proposal from Pia, they both started meeting on a regular basis almost every alternate day. They used to meet at each other's residence, coffee house, food joints, pubs and everywhere to spend some quality time together.

Their meetings began as usual, they got to know about each other much more and better. Pia used to bunk her college lectures to meet Ray. She started making excuses from her parents for being late in evenings.

They both had visited numerous food joints and pubs during the first six months of their relationship. Sagar Ratna, Bercos, Karims, Cafe Coffee Day, Barista, Chinos, Empire are some of them I can quickly recall.

Select City Walk, DLF Place Saket, MGF Metropolitan, DT City Center, Great India Place, Centerstage Mall, Spice Mall... they both have visited almost every mall located in the tri - city of Delhi - Gurgaon - Noida.

Their relationship blossomed as a flower blooms in the spring season, like rain drop becomes a Pearl in the oyster. Everyone around them was in surprise... how within a few months they have such a strong bonding... they know each other so well... they don't have to use words to express themselves to each other...

They were so much into each other, they never bothered about what others have to say for or against them. They could talk to each other for hours ... they could text each other nonstop and could stare at each other without a blink for long hours.

Their love was unconditional for each other, and surprisingly none had expectations from the other. I remember a few of their interesting meetings which they both shared with me secretly (not supposedly to be shared with anyone, but I ll share with you).

I do not remember the dates, but yes I do remember the incidents that happened and brought both of them too close to each other to be separated.

The first movie they watched together was Vicky Donor, which cherished their love a bit more. Ray started singing Pia's favourite song from the movie, "Pani da rang... vekh ke... ankhiyanch hanju rudd de" and Pia would lose herself to that melodious voice. The song complemented their romance so well, that Pia would call up Ray at 3 in the morning to listen to the song from him.

Then came Ray's birthday and Pia had planned a trip of theirs which got cancelled at the last moment and she had stayed back at Ray's place. It was a national holiday and shops were shut. Pia reached Ray's place in the morning and stayed there for the next three days. Those three days were full of love, romance and fun for both of them. They went for lunch outside, flew kites in the evening, sipped a cup of tea on the terrace, watched a movie, had dinner from the same platter and went for a night walk together. They partied, got drunk, danced, got clicked, smoked, cooked food, got drenched in rain, sung romantic numbers, and spent evenings together sitting closest to each other.

These were the moments which strengthened their relationship further to an extent of treating each other as spouses. Their dates became more regular and intense. By this time, they had started discussing their cultures and families to make the other one comfortable with the differences.

Their next interesting meeting was on Pia's birthday which was a surprise celebration at Ray's place. Pia had come down to Noida for an official meeting, after which she went to meet Ray, where she decided to stay back so that she could celebrate her birthday with the person she loves the most. She called up her parents and told them that her friends have planned a surprise birthday party for her and that she would not be able to come back. After some arguments, her parents agreed.

Ray ordered her choice of flavour for the birthday cake, her favourite food and loads of alcohol. Alcohol has been the major inclusion of their parties and their story. Pia had never enjoyed her birthday so much before, since no one has made her feel so special before. She danced with his friends, she confessed her love for him, and had the best moments with her love of life.

Bored of her new job, Pia changed her workplace within a week of joining. And accepted an offer of Marketing Executive with a hospitality brand in Delhi. To work smoothly she shifted to Delhi, close to her workplace and Noida. She hardly stayed there in the PG, rather she would travel daily to her work from Noida to spend more and more time with her beloved. She skipped her office to take care of her partner, and cooked food. She enjoyed every moment of her life she spent with the love of her life...

CHAPTER FIVE

CAUGHT BY CHANCE

Everything was going smooth, Pia and Ray both were very happy in their own dreamland. When, their meetings and Pia's night stay at Ray's place, came to the knowledge of the former's parents.

After shifting to Delhi, Pia used to visit her parents on weekends. But that day, she did not want to leave Ray and wanted to spend more time with him. She made an excuse that she is having severe backache and would not be able to travel, therefore would come the next day i.e. Sunday. Her parents had some doubt but did not counter question her. She spent that night with Ray at his place.

To her destiny, her phone's battery got discharged and she was not carrying the charger. To know her well, her parents called up at the landline number of the PG, from where they got to know that she left PG the day before yesterday for her home.

Pia somehow managed to charge her phone's battery and switched it on the very moment. She was watching her favourite movie "The Notebook" while Ray was resting. Her life and the movie both were flowing in sync. She got a call from her parents to know her whereabouts. She maintained her reply and told them she is at her PG. After a few minutes, she again got a call from her mother, shouting and yelling at her that she knows her whereabouts and is surprised to learn about her lies. That was the moment in the movie, when Allie's parents get to know that she is with Noah at his place...

Nervous Pia wakes up Ray and tells him the entire episode. He tells her to go back home and make her parents understand the situation. Pia left Ray's place and boarded the train then metro to reach her home.

On reaching her home, she has to face her parents' anger and yellings. Her mother asks her if she has slept with him even, frightened Pia says, "Mom, I know my limits". The next day, Pia's dad dropped her to her workplace and while on return she took back with her, the entire luggage which she had brought to the PG.

Now, everyday Pia is accompanied by her dad to her office and then back to home. They ask her to forget Ray, but she pleads with them that he is her life. She would not be happy with anyone else.

Days, weeks passed by Pia has now changed her job and moved to a small advertising agency in Malviya Nagar. Though it's her new job, she still took ample leaves to meet Ray almost every week. Their parties, meetings and coffee were still on the same pace.

Pia's new job had a little bit of fieldwork as well. She had to attend seminars, exhibitions and events to get new clientele on board. So, she quickly used to wrap up her visits and then meet Ray.

Their meetings increased, their love intensified, their commitment to each other strengthened. I used to feel jealous at times also, thinking about the bond and affection for each other. For me they were inseparable. But destiny had some other plans for them.

CHAPTER SIX

LOVE OR MISTAKE

In her new job, Pia was quite happy and satisfied as she had a good time to spend with Ray during her field visits. One of her colleagues, Sandhya, used to accompany her sometimes halfway to Ray's place. They together planned a trip to Manali also. It was Ray - Pia and Sandhya - Sandeep (Her love interest). I remember, Pia was so happy for the trip. She told me how they both (Ray and Pia) had spent the best time of their lifetimes together. They cuddled and snuggled within each other. Played in snow, walked around hand – in – hand, went on a shopping spree and partied together. This trip of their got them really very close. They were into each other's arms, being able to feel heartbeats. Ray's first kiss on the forehead assured Pia of their togetherness. Their love intensified with each kiss and their craving of loving each other. That night Pia and Ray rose to love falling for each other.

Next morning, Pia was little nervous but Ray assured her that they would always be together come what may. Days, weeks and then months passed by; Pia got worried as she suspected pregnancy! She went through self-test kits, however the results were negative. Pia started gaining weight and started worrying about her health and then one day she went for a check-up with her dad...

The news came as a shocker for Pia... Doctor informed her that she is 5 months pregnant... yes 5 Months. Her dad was called in and he got the biggest shock of his life. Uncle and Pia left the hospital and went straight to their home. At home, aunty was there all annoyed and agitated; she slapped Pia at once without any hesitation. Pia stood there silently as she had no words to say and she was all lost in some another world. I still wonder what thoughts were troubling her while all this was going on in her life.

Pia's parents got her to abort her child. The family went through lot of pain. Pia seemed lost, she did not have any idea as to what is happening, why this is happening and how she landed up in this mess of her life. Ray was nowhere, no phone calls, no messages, no emails...

After 3 months, Ray contacted Pia and apologized for not being there when she needed him the most. Pia loved him so much that she just melted with his few words. They met again after 4 months of the episode. Pia had recovered physically, however was still struggling emotionally and mentally. Ray expressed his concerns and tells Pia to talk to her parents and convince them about their relationship. Pia agrees and leaves for her home...

CHAPTER SEVEN

THE LAST MEETING

After weeks of efforts, Pia was successful at convincing her parents to meet Ray once and then decide if he is a suitable match for her or not. Pia's father was not willing to meet Ray, however just for the sake of Pia he agreed. He took Pia's grand parents also with him to meet Ray. Everyone questioned Ray about his education, family, career plans and his intentions to marry Pia. After a long session of 2 hours they all left for home. Dada jee expressed his thoughts, "Munda changa hai par karda kuch ni. Te punjabi wi ni hega. Munde de parents wi zada padhe likhe ni haige, saadi kudi nu kiven samjhange?" Now dad shared his opinion, "mujhe nahi pasand, bas. Main haan nahi kar sakta."

Pia was left with no choice but to wait for another chance to talk to her parents one last time about Ray. Meanwhile, she grabbed a job opportunity in a startup. While she was enjoying her work life, she also had Ray in her life. One day she thought of pursuing further studies, so this way she will be able to buy some more time from her parents for the wedlock. She started looking for institutions in and outside India.

Her friends helped her make decision and she decided upon a college in London. She told her parents, and they were happy of the thought that this way she would realize how wrong she was in choosing Ray for herself. They agreed and started preparing for her new journey. Pia had to restrict her meetings with Ray so she could prepare documents and other legal formalities.

Now Pia and Ray met only twice a month. Few days before leaving for London, Pia and Ray spent entire day together. Ray showed his concerns that this long distance might ruin their relationship. Pia assured him of nothing such sort of things would affect their relation. She would always take some time out to talk to Ray and vice-versa.

Finally the day came, Pia bid adieu to her family and boarded the flight to London. Ray was standing at a distance to bid bye to his lover, unable to gather strength to come and meet Pia before she leaves the country. He wanted to cuddle her and tell her that he loves a lot and will wait till eternity for her to come back and be his for lifetime.

Pia saw him in tears but could not do much. She moved forward towards airport entry gates and got busy with the travel formalities. One last time, she made a call to Ray, saying, “Goodbye, hope to see you soon. Don’t miss me and take care”. These words somehow hurt Ray and he could not understand if this is the END or the NEW Beginning for both Ray and Pia...

Printed by Libri Plureos GmbH in Hamburg,
Germany